DORA HAD A LITTLE LAMB

adapted by Elle D. Risco
based on the teleplay by Eric Weiner
illustrated by Steven Savitsky

ADVANCE
PUBLISHERS

Based on the TV series Dora the Explorer® as seen on Nick Jr.®

Advance Publishers, L.C.
1060 Maitland Center Commons, Suite 365
Maitland, FL 32751 USA

10 9 8 7 6 5 4 3 2 1
ISBN-10: 1-57973-369-7

¡Hola! *Soy* Dora, and this is my friend Boots! We found *The Big Book of Nursery Rhymes*! Do you see who is on the cover?

¡*Sí! El corderito*—the little lamb from "Mary Had a Little Lamb." Little Lamb is sad because she can't find Mary. Don't worry, Little Lamb! We can help you!

Will you help us bring Little Lamb back to Mary? Great! Come on! ¡*Vámonos!*

We need to follow Little Lamb into *The Big Book of Nursery Rhymes* so we can look for Mary. *¡Mira!* There's Jack and the Beanstalk and the Old Woman Who Lives in a Shoe.

But how will we find Mary's House? Who do we ask for help when we don't know which way to go?

Map! Will you check Map and find out how to get to Mary's House? You have to say "Map!"

Map says first we need to go past the Water Spout. Then we jump all the way over the Moon. And that's how we'll get to Mary's House.
Where do we go first? The Water Spout, yeah! Come on! *¡Vámonos!*

Look! Do you see the stars? We need to catch them! Reach up and catch the stars. Reach up, up, up!

Good catching! We caught all of the stars—even Glowy, the Bright-Light Explorer Star! Let's put the stars in the Star Pocket.

Let's bring Little Lamb to Mary and find more nursery rhymes as we go!

Hickory, dickory, dock. Do you see the mouse that ran up the clock? How about Jack and his candlestick? And where is Little Miss Muffet, eating her curds and whey? *¿Dónde está?*

There's Peter Piper! He is going to pick some pickled peppers. Peter Piper wants to pick enough pickled peppers so that everyone can have one. Let's count how many of us there are.

Uno, dos, tres, cuatro, cinco, seis, siete. So how many pickled peppers do we need? Seven!

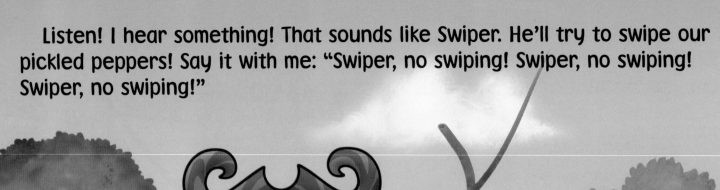

Listen! I hear something! That sounds like Swiper. He'll try to swipe our pickled peppers! Say it with me: "Swiper, no swiping! Swiper, no swiping! Swiper, no swiping!"

Yay! We stopped Swiper. Now we can eat our pickled peppers. *¡Son deliciosos!* They're delicious! Now let's keep going and bring Little Lamb back to Mary!

We made it to the Water Spout. But look! The Water Spout is turned on and there's water everywhere! We need to turn it off so we can get by.

Do you see someone who can climb up the Water Spout? *¡Sí!* The Itsy Bitsy Spider!

¡Fantástico! The Itsy Bitsy Spider climbed up the Water Spout and turned off the water! Where do we go next on our way to Mary's House? Yeah! The Moon! We need to go over the Moon!

But wait! I think I see someone who needs our help. It's Humpty Dumpty! And it looks like he's just had a great fall!

Boots and I help Humpty Dumpty back onto the wall!

There is *la luna*! We made it to the Moon. Now we have to jump *over* the Moon.

Hey, diddle, diddle, the cat in the fiddle. Who jumped over the Moon? The Cow! *¡La vaca!* She can give us a ride over the Moon!

The Cow speaks Spanish. To get the Cow to jump, we say " *¡Salta!* "

Thanks for saying, "*¡Salta!*" We made it over *la luna*.

Wow, it's very dark out here over the Moon! We need something—or someone—to light our way back down. Who can help us light our way? *¡Sí!* Glowy Star!

Whew! We made it back down to the ground. Look! There's Mary's House! It's so far away. The three boys in a tub can give us a ride.

Whoa! We zoomed through a mud puddle. Now we're all dirty! Little Lamb's fleece isn't white as snow anymore!

We need to get Little Lamb clean. Will you check Backpack and find something we can *all* use to get clean?

Yay! Little Lamb is clean—and we made it to Mary's House! Mary and Little Lamb are so happy to see each other. They never want to lose each other again. From now on, everywhere that Mary goes, Little Lamb will be sure to go too!

We did it! *¡Lo hicimos!* We brought Little Lamb to Mary's House!
We couldn't have done it without you! *¡Gracias!* Thanks for helping!